The Tale of Gus the Grumbly Grizzly

Terri Wiltshire

ILLUSTRATED BY
Rebecca Archer

Kingfisher Books

NEW YORK

There was a secret meeting in the forest. The animals were very worried. Gus the Grizzly was in a foot-stomping, ground-shaking bad mood.

Gus made growly-scowly faces. He made grumbly-grouchy noises. "This will not do," said the animals. "We must think of a plan."

"We'll give Gus a gift,"
the animals decided.
"I have a shiny rock
from the river," said the beaver.
"That should please him."

But when the animals
showed Gus their shiny gift,
he sniffed and snarled
in a grumbly-mumbly way.

"Maybe Gus is hungry,"
the animals thought.
"I have the best collection
of berries and nuts in the forest,"
said the little raccoon. "That
should cheer him up."

But when the animals brought Gus the berries and nuts, he moaned and groaned in a grumbly-mumbly way.

"Gus must be cold,"
the animals guessed.
"I'll weave a blanket of ferns
and flowers," said the squirrel.
"That should make him
warm and happy."

But when the animals placed the blanket on his shoulders, Gus drooped and moped in a grumbly-mumbly way.

The animals couldn't agree.
They fretted and they frowned.
They bellowed and they
stamped their feet.
Only Baby Rabbit knew
what to do.

The animals stopped their shouting. They couldn't believe their eyes. Gus the Grizzly was chuckling and giggling and gurgling with glee.

Baby Rabbit knew all along what would make Gus a happy Grizzly. A side-splitting, grumbly-busting bear hug. And that's just what she gave him!

KINGFISHER BOOKS
Grisewood & Dempsey Inc.
95 Madison Avenue,
New York, New York 10016

First American edition 1993
2 4 6 8 10 9 7 5 3 1
Copyright text and illustrations © 1993 Cedarwood Press

Library of Congress Cataloging-in-Publication Data
Wiltshire, Terri
The tale of Gus the grumbly grizzly/Terri Wiltshire:
[illustrated by] Rebecca Archer, — 1st American ed.
p. cm. — (Kingfisher foldouts)
Summary: The animals are not able to cheer up grumbly Gus the
grizzly. The cover folds out to provide a backdrop for the story.
1. Toy and movable books — Specimens. [1. Bears — Fiction.
2. Animals — Fiction. 3. Toy and movable books.] I. Archer
Rebecca, ill. II. Title. III. Series.
PZ7.W6997Tag 1993
[E] — dc20 92-46248 CIP AC

ISBN 1-85697-856-7
Printed in Hong Kong